DEAR OLD DOGS

DEAR OLD DOGS
Gwen Head

atmosphere press

*This novel is dedicated to the real "Debbie"
I adopted from a dog academy,
and to the people and animals affected by
the devastation of Hurricane Harvey.*

1

She woke to glass breaking. Jumping out of bed, Kit put on the robe she had discarded at the foot of the bed. It was probably just a raccoon or a cat knocking over the trash she put on the back porch after Clare left. She hadn't wanted to carry it all the way to the alley.

Tonight she hadn't turned on the outside sensor lights that flooded the circumference of the house when something got near. They were so bright; it was hard for the neighbors to sleep when a cat tripped them on in the middle of the night.

She flipped the master switch in her bedroom. She didn't want to call the police until she was sure what was happening. Kit had heavy drapes covering most of the windows in the house. Her master suite was next to the kitchen. She was quietly tip-toeing to the back door. Kit could see the outline of a man through the transparent curtain. He was rattling the doorknob and pushing on the door.

"Who's there?" Nothing.

"One more time before I call the police, who's there?" Nothing.

"Okay, you asked for it." Kit's cellphone had somehow materialized in her hand. She didn't remember putting it in the pocket of her robe last night. She dialed 911 and told the dispatcher that someone was trying to get in her back door.

"Hold on Kit, we're coming. It will be two minutes flat. Cecil is patrolling tonight and he's one mile away. Just stay on the line with me. It can't be much longer."

Soon, Cecil was at the front door banging on it with his flashlight. "Kit, it's me, Cecil Park."

Kit hurried to the front door while still talking to the dispatcher on her cell phone. She opened the door, saying, "Someone's trying to come in my back door."

"Okay, I'm going to circle around the house. Where's the gate?" Kit told him it was on the north side of the house.

She hurried back through the house. Cecil said loudly, "SIR, PLEASE STEP BACK FROM THE DOOR. HANDS ON YOUR HEAD AND GET ON YOUR KNEES, NOW!"

Everything happened so fast, she wasn't sure exactly what had transpired. Cecil had handcuffed Ken Swift outside her back door. He didn't know where he was or why he was being handcuffed. Cecil and the officers that responded to the call immediately realized something wasn't right with this man. They led him back around to the front yard to wait on the ambulance.

He was in his pajamas. Ken lived two blocks west of her on Silver Elm Street. She vaguely remembered him and his wife from some functions years ago. Cecil told Kit that Eleanor, his wife, had been called. She had been asleep and didn't understand why Ken was in Kit's backyard.

Kit told Cecil, after they put the disoriented Ken in the ambulance, "I won't be pressing charges. I just want him to get the medical attention he needs."

He kept trying to get up, saying, "I want to go home." Eleanor arrived and got in the back of the ambulance. Kit could see Eleanor through the back windows. She was stroking Ken's forehead and saying something Kit knew would be soft and endearing.

Cecil was leaving. "Kit you need an alarm system and maybe a dog to boot."

"Yes, I think you're right."

*

Her name was Katherine Carson; her father had tagged her with the nickname of Kit. He loved the old Kit Carson western movies; they had watched many together on Saturdays. He told her she was a trailblazer and an Indian fighter.

"Kit," he would say, putting his arm around her, "with your name and courage, you can accomplish anything you set your mind to."

She grew up in a small Central Texas town named Evansville, population 70,000. She inherited her family's home in 1972 when her parents were killed in a car accident while vacationing in Colorado. Kit had been in her twenties, single, and didn't have a clue what she wanted to do with her life. She had gone into real estate, but she always felt it wasn't her true calling in life.

She stayed with real estate for twenty-five years, retired, no children, never married and did it her way, so to speak. Kit was now in her mid-sixties. She had saved her money during her productive years in real estate, and her parents had left her a modest inheritance. She put the question out there every time she thought about purchasing something: "Do I need this, or do I just want it?" It had saved her from being frivolous.

*

The next morning, with only two hours of sleep, Kit called Clare to tell her what had happened while she made coffee. Cecil had called earlier to tell her the doctor said Ken had a stroke.

"Clare, I would like to go visit Ken in the hospital or, at least, talk to Eleanor and tell her how sorry I am and ask if there's anything I can do to help."

"Okay, I can do that with you."

"Clare, getting old isn't for wimps."

Soon, they were headed to the hospital. Clare said, "We are all facing the same thing as we age. At least you and I have each other to call and check to make sure everything's okay. It's important."

Eleanor was sitting in the waiting room crying softly. Kit sat down beside her with Clare on the other side.

Kit put her arms around her, "It's going to be alright. Is there anything we can do for you? Do you need us to check on your house? I can bring you something to eat?"

Eleanor looked emotionally drained and fragile, "No, our son Dan is coming. The doctor said Ken may get better, but if that doesn't happen, we need to discuss a facility that can help with his needs. This is just horrible. I'm sorry for everything that happened. Our world is spinning out of control, and I don't know what to do about it."

Kit assured her, "No need, just take care of your family. If I can do anything to help, please don't hesitate to call me."

Kit gave her a personal card with all her information on it. She and Clare left when Eleanor's son appeared.

Kit asked Clare if she had a little time before they went back to her house.

"Yes, of course. Do you want to get something to eat?"

"Yes, but first I want to pick out a dog at the shelter. It's time."

Clare told Kit that David, her brother, had adopted a dog from the The Guardian Academy outside of town. Kit had seen the weekly newspaper advertisements.

"David explained it to me a couple of months ago," Clare said. "He adopted a German Shepard named Bishoff-Star. The Academy is a renowned dog-training facility for student trainers that come from all over the world to train. When they graduate in 9 weeks, they can start their own business. David said the student trainers go to the Humane Society in Evansville and pick a dog to go through training with them. When the student trainer graduates, the dog is adoptable and goes back to the shelter. The dogs are spayed or neutered, a GPS chip is surgically placed between their shoulder blades, and they are kept up-to-date with all their shots. You would only have to pay the adoption fee from the shelter."

Kit had always wanted a dog that had been trained, a pet that would listen when she said, "Stay, sit, and down." This seemed like the perfect solution, so she and Clare made a plan to head to the Academy.

That day, as they drove, they passed a large sign that said, "Oh, Behave!" The next sign said, "30 acres with agility runs through the woods, swimming pool, gymnasium for individual training and group sessions. Call 1-800-999-BARK."

They turned down a dirt road lined with pecan trees; the lane looked so lush. Turning into the large parking lot, they saw an above-ground swimming pool where two dogs, one large and one small, were jumping in as two women commanded. There were various fenced-in areas where trainers had their dogs running after balls or going through commands. Kit and Clare had never seen anything like this.

There was an arrow pointing to the office and Pro Dog Shop. They walked into a large room that smelled like pet supplies. There was a large screen TV on the wall behind the receptionist's counter showing a video of a German Shepard running an obstacle course. They both said at the same time, "Bishoff?"

The receptionist approached them, saying, "Hi, I'm Betty, may I help you?"

Kit said she was interested in adopting a dog. Betty talked on the phone and told Kit and Clare someone would be there shortly to talk with them. They looked around at all the dog toys. Kit particularly liked the balls where owners could put treats in the hollow space. The pet would lick and play with the toy all day while the owner was away. In a large glass cooler, they could see fresh buffalo, chicken, lamb, and beef dog food. They had pallets of dry dog food along the back wall for the small, medium, and large dogs in 10, 20 and 40 lb. bags. They also had a small cooler with soy ice cream and fresh dog treats for training or rewarding your pet. Along another wall were collars and leashes.

They turned around and saw the big screen TV behind the counter showing dogs in various training exercises on the grounds. The video flashed on a large suite for two dogs, where your dogs could stay together while you were away. The dogs in the suite were watching a big screen TV video of various dogs and their trainers going through training commands.

Clare commented, "I can see where that might be entertaining for your pets."

A man walked up. "Hello, my name is Luke Mitchell, how may I help you?"

"My name is Kit Carson, and this is my friend Clare Bishop. Her brother, David, adopted a German Shepard named Bishoff-Star from here a couple of months ago. That's how I found out about The Guardian Academy."

"Yes, I remember Bishoff-Star, a great dog. No other dog has shown his ability on the agility runs. He was one of our best. Tell me what you are looking for in a pet? A large, medium, or small dog, and trained for what duties?"

"Well, it's for me," Kit said. "I had someone try to open my back door a couple of nights ago, and I figured it was time for me to adopt a pet companion. I like large dogs. I had a Lab for fourteen years."

"I think we might have a breed that you will enjoy and would make a good guard dog for you. Come with me." Luke led them to the gymnasium across from the pro shop. "You both can sit on the bleachers, and I will call someone to bring the first dog I would like you to meet. The trainer will take her through the commands and bring the dog in front of you. Pet her if you like. If not, then we will introduce you to the next dog."

Kit and Clare sat on the bleachers watching other dogs at the back of the gym go through commands. Some were jumping over low poles; others were running through large tubes and agility runs. A few dogs were laying on trampoline-style (two x three feet) beds. The beds were cute and kept the dogs off the floor. She could see they would be comfortable, but where would she put it?

Luke sat on an office roll-around chair. He scooted close in front of them. He explained that the beds were for training and time-out for the dogs. He said, "See the Dalmatian at the back with her trainer? Watch."

Luke called out, "Lisa, take Mitzi to her training bed and walk away."

Doing as they both were told, Mitzi got on the training bed, and Lisa gave the hand signal for "stay" and walked away. Mitzi stayed on the training bed; she crawled to the very edge with her paws hanging over slightly. She intensely watched Lisa walk all the way around the gymnasium, but her paws never touched the floor. Lisa walked back around to Mitzi. They had not taken their eyes off each other.

"Good girl!" Lisa gave her a treat out of the pouch around her waist.

Mitzi stepped one foot off the bed and Lisa corrected her. Mitzi stepped back and laid down again, watching Lisa's face, ready for the next command.

The double doors opened, and a large black dog with no tail walked in slightly behind a male trainer.

"Oh my god, Clare, she's beautiful." She had a brindle butt and feet, but all the rest of her was black.

Kit asked, "What is she?"

Luke told her she was a Rottweiler/Mastiff breed, six years old, who loved everyone and everyone loved her. Student trainers were passing by and they all said, "Hi Debbie." She wagged her nub in acknowledgement, but all her hundred or so pounds were focused on her trainer. He took her around the gym and back in front of them.

Her trainer introduced himself as Gordy. He said he was from New York and had picked Debbie at the shelter in Evansville to go through his training with him. She would be here for two more weeks, and then Gordy would be graduating, going back home as a certified professional dog trainer. If no one adopted Debbie during the next two weeks, she would go back to the shelter, trained and adoptable.

Kit had never owned a dog of this caliber and power. Her Lab, Bessta, had been a high energy dog, and she could be rambunctious, but this might be something totally different. She didn't want a mean dog but one that would get the point across if need be. The other night, Ken had proved to her that she was very vulnerable and exposed.

Gordy brought Debbie to Kit and said, "You may pet her if you like." Kit put the palm of her hand up to Debbie's nose. Debbie licked her palm; Kit was sold.

"Luke, you have been very kind. I can see that Debbie knows her commands, and she would guard me and our home. Would I get a lesson with her?"

"Yes, you would get her exit lesson after student graduation as her new owner. Think about it tonight, Kit. If you decide not Debbie, then I do have a couple others you might be interested in adopting. If you decided to go for it, then go to the shelter outside of town and fill out the adoption papers, especially before she leaves here, as you might not get another chance before someone else adopts her.

Kit and Clare followed Gordy and Debbie back to her cage. Once in, Kit talked directly to Debbie and put her fingers between the wire, "I'm coming back to get you Debbie."

Debbie wagged her nub and put a warm wet tongue to Kit's fingers.

"OK then, I'll be back." Kit knew at that moment she and Debbie had connected.

Kit believed when someone rescued an animal and looked into their eyes, meaning their kindness and love for that animal, they awakened their soul. With that knowledge, she believed humans took on the responsibility of nurturing the well-being of that animal.

Clare got in the car and turned to Kit with concern on her face. "Are you sure, Kit? That's a lot of dog."

Kit was smiling. "Yes, she is—and adorable too. Her big warm tongue licking my hand got me."

That night Kit was excited about Debbie. She hadn't realized how badly she wanted a new pet companion, a new family member. Kit cleaned the house in anticipation of her newfound friend, and that's exactly what she would be to her. Kit would have someone to talk to again, someone to follow her around the house. It would be a long two weeks.

Kit stayed busy, and nothing eventful happened. She'd finally gotten the alarm system installed. Kit called Eleanor to ask about Ken. So far, he still didn't recognize Eleanor or their son, Dan.

Eleanor had Ken transferred from the hospital to Starry Night's Family Home. She said she didn't think he knew the difference. She had an attorney and her son helping to get their finances in order. Ken's name would be taken off all titles, as this is what Eleanor was told had to be done. Thank goodness Ken had turned sixty-five a couple of months ago, as Medicare would kick in and his family would have health insurance for him. Kit knew this must be a difficult time of adjustment for Eleanor and Dan.

2

Kit was making coffee, humming to herself, with Debbie on her mind. Today was the day. Debbie's trainer was graduating that morning, and Kit had an appointment at 11 o'clock to take her lesson and bring her new friend home.

David and Clare picked her up; they were her support system, should she need it. Kit believed that sometimes a person had to take a leap-of-faith about new experiences, and this was her time. All seemed good. David and Clare seemed to think so, too.

David had told Kit that the training bed hadn't worked out for Bishoff. It took up too much room, and Bishoff had continuously whined, wanting to follow David around the house. David took the training bed back, and everyone was happy.

Clare had a Siamese cat, Annie that she swore growled and would attack if anyone tried to come in her house without being invited. Annie had always been nice to Kit, and Kit was nice back.

They went a little early to the Academy pet store for the pronged collar and a leash. Kit also wanted to try the buffalo dog food and treats. David had said the treats were great, and for a while the pronged collar would let them get acquainted with each other.

Kit picked out a heavy-duty red collar at the pet store. It would be the one she would wear all the time at home with her tags attached. She also bought a pronged collar with a matching leash. The pronged collar she picked out had a red nylon strap that stretched, so she could put it over Debbie's head without hitting her in the eye with a prong and then snap it back together. Gordy had told her the pronged collar was for both of their safeties until they got to know each other.

"Be confident and be her leader," Gordy expressed to her.

Kit knew this to be true; she could see where a dog the size of Debbie could easily drag a senior person into the street after seeing some critter.

Kit was nervous and excited while they waited for Gordy to bring Debbie to the trainer's floor one last time before he left and went back home to New York. Gordy and Debbie made their appearance through the double doors. Debbie was walking the 'Rottweiler Swagger', staying one step behind Gordy. He told her to sit and, pretty as you please, she backed up a step and sat down. He told her, "Stay Debbie," dropped the leash, walked away twenty or thirty steps, turned, waited thirty seconds, then called her to him.

Gordy told her he was so proud, "Good girl Debbie!" He gave her a treat from his pouch. This was how the dogs were rewarded; they got a treat from their trainer's pouch.

Gordy walked her back in front of Kit and placed the leash in her hand. He said his goodbyes to Debbie and shook Luke's hand.

"Good luck, Kit. She will be your best friend; she loves her kisses, treats, and retrieving a ball."

Gordy said his plane left at 2 o'clock and walked out the gymnasium door to go pack and pick up his dog that came with him to the school. He had been living at the facilities provided there on the grounds. Kit had noticed the three RVs parked and hooked-up outside.

Debbie looked a little lost, standing there, looking after Gordy. Luke told Kit to walk Debbie around the gymnasium.

"Make her stay one step behind you. Keep your talking to a minimum as you walk. If she moves ahead of you, make her stop and sit, then make a complete circle with her until she comes around again. Then start forward again with her one step behind, making the correction."

Kit and Debbie walked together, both with their heads up high. She stopped when Kit told her. She and Kit went through all her commands perfectly.

"This is great fun," she said to Clare and David as they passed the bleachers. The next time around, Kit stopped in front of Luke. "We are one," she laughed. "I think we can go home now."

Luke reminded Kit that if it didn't work out for some reason, she was to take Debbie back to the shelter, not here. Kit shook her head no.

Kit and Debbie got in the back seat. Debbie gave her lots of kisses on the way home. She was happy she had made this decision. David and Clare left, telling her to call and let them know how it was going that evening.

Debbie had been fed and given water. It was now or never. Kit put on Debbie's pronged collar and leash. She was a little nervous about walking Debbie down the street, but there was no turning back. She wanted to introduce Debbie to everyone on her street. "Be confident," she said to herself as they walked out the front door.

Three weeks passed quickly for them both, as their routine formed and continued to grow. Debbie wanted to be fed and let outside by 6:00 am, and then and only then would she get on her bed again to take a morning nap while Kit drank coffee.

Texas temperatures in August were still in the nineties, so they didn't get out much during the heat of the day. Kit had started looking into "Pet Friendly" hotels and motels online. Why couldn't she and Debbie go on a trip just staying at those places? She had no doubt that the managers would see how well-trained Debbie was and let them rent for the night.

Another week passed with ease as she and Debbie tried every few days to go somewhere new and different in the cool of the mornings. That day, Kit was taking her to the small Evansville Lake outside of town. It would be a test to see if Debbie ran away or would come back to her. They got ready. Debbie knew she was going somewhere, so she got her nub going as fast as she could. Kit made her sit before they went in the garage to get in the car. She had bought Debbie a breast collar that would allow Kit to buckle her in the seat belt. If something happened, if someone ran into her, Debbie would have a seat belt holding her.

If all went well, Kit thought they would be ready to take a trip. They drove to the marina where the pickups backed down to the water to launch their boats. Kit had picked Tuesday because most men were working and not out on the water. All-in-all, the day was fun, and Debbie got all the exercise she needed. Only once did she go after three ducks that got too close. Nothing bad had happened. Kit whistled, and Debbie came bounding out of the water. She brought a large towel to dry Debbie before she got in the car. She knew now that wherever they went, it had to have a lake. Debbie loved the water.

*

She kept busy during the week planning the trip. Kit thought a short trip to a rental cottage outside of Kerrville, Texas would be good. She would call and book the cottage at the Heart of Texas Cottages. She and Debbie would be able to wander the back roads of Kerrville and Bandera. Pets were welcome, it said on the web site, for an extra charge of twenty-five dollars a night. They would stay two nights.

The next morning Kit took Debbie for a walk at the mall. She didn't know how Debbie would react to traveling on the road and taking care of business. It would be easier going through towns if there were signs giving directions to a park, but that wasn't always possible. The walk would be a test run to see how well Debbie followed Kit's commands.

The east side of the mall by the theater had more green space. It was seven o'clock, and the stores didn't open until 10. Kit parked and opened the back door to unclick Debbie from the seat belt, but before she could back out of the car, Debbie jumped past her and took off.

Kit was calling her name, "Debbie stop! STOP DEBBIE!" If Kit could have gotten close to Debbie's leash, she would have stepped on it and brought her to a halt.

Debbie's nose was to the ground tracking something. She stopped to gobble part of an old hot dog someone had thrown on the ground. Kit made her move, stepping on the leash. Debbie sat and looked up at Kit while finishing her morsel.

Kit felt the incident was her fault. She should have told Debbie to "STAY" until she was ready to get her out of the car.

"Come on, let's go home."

Debbie was more than willing to be led back to the car after her mid-day snack. Kit felt a little uneasy; what would she do the next time Debbie got away from her? What if it was in another town while they were traveling? When she got home, she called the Academy and told them what had happened. They told her to bring Debbie to the Academy for a refresher course. A group session of owners was planned for nine in the morning.

*

The sky was bright blue and not a cloud in sight. She could smell a whiff of autumn in the morning air. They walked into the large gymnasium for their lesson. Debbie was overly excited and wanted to chase a ball someone had thrown.

Kit brought her back in line, saying, "Sit." Debbie sat, but Kit could tell she was still thinking about the ball. Kit took Debbie in a circle and started off again towards the group.

Dogs and their owners were in various positions of commands.

The trainer clapped her hands, "Okay people, let's get in a circle with your pets and bring them to a sitting position."

Luke came over to Kit and wanted to speak to her in private. They stepped over to the set of bleachers.

"Did I do something wrong?" she asked.

"No, we have a special request from the Sheriff's Department."

Sheriff Lute Turner came to stand in front of Kit. Debbie was looking up at the Sheriff from her sitting position.

"Hello Kit. We have a situation in town that I think Debbie might be able to help us."

"Okay, I will try. What's going on?"

"Last night someone murdered eighty-three year old Rebecca Lambert at her residence. I called the Academy this morning trying to find a dog that has an extraordinary sense of smell. They told me you were coming in today for a class and that Debbie had shown that kind of tracking ability when she was here at the academy. We would like to see if she could help us. We don't have a scent dog available."

"Sure, Sheriff."

"Alright, we would like to take Debbie to Mrs. Lambert's house. The murderer dropped his handkerchief in the front yard. It's okay if she doesn't pick up on the scent. We thought we would try. Is that agreeable with you?"

"Okay, can I take Debbie in my car and follow you?"

"Sure thing."

She followed the Sheriff's car to the address. She didn't really want to be involved, but if there was anything she could do to help, she felt like she should try. She prayed most of the way for guidance and for protection over Debbie. She didn't want anything to happen to her pet companion, her odd little family of two.

Kit got Debbie out of the car. They walked with Sheriff Turner to a group of deputies waiting in the front yard. Debbie sensed a foreboding of evil near and stayed close to her master.

One of the deputies brought the handkerchief to Sheriff Turner. He pulled it out of the plastic bag and let Debbie smell. She stood and started for the street. The deputies and Sheriff started after her. Debbie was on her mission; she knew what was expected. Kit was having a hard time keeping up with Debbie at her steady trot, but she didn't want to let go of her leash.

Two blocks down, Debbie stopped at a door that led to the stairwell of an older, brick apartment building downtown. The Sheriff held up his hand, signaling Kit to stop, stand back and let them secure the entrance.

They gave her the 'go' and up the stairs they went. Debbie stopped at apartment number four and sat down. The Sheriff pointed for Kit to go back down the stairs and outside to wait. The door was closing after her when she heard the Sheriff knock on the door.

"It's the Sheriff's department, open the door." No one answered. "Roddy, go get the Super with his key to this apartment."

The Sheriff knocked again. "Open the door, it's the Sheriff's Department."

She and Debbie hurried outside and around the building just in case something went down. She wanted them away from harm.

The Superintendent had the master key and started up the stairs when they heard glass breaking in the apartment.

"Sheriff?" The Deputy asked.

"Yeah, Roddy." He pointed at the Super, "Who lives here?"

"A man named John Weiss had lived there for three days," he replied.

The Sheriff moved to the left of the door "Come on out John!" Nothing.

They heard scuffling and a yell when the man jumped from the window. The Sheriff hoped he had sustained enough injuries that he couldn't get away fast.

The Super opened the door; Sheriff Turner rushed to the window while Roddy cleared the apartment. Debbie had backed the man up against the wall. He had received injuries to his leg in the fall. Debbie had a low, almost-silent growl as she faced-off with him, daring him to move, her hackles standing straight up.

Soon after, Sheriff Turner buckled Debbie in the back seat, patting her on the head and saying, "You did good today Debbie, you got the bad guy."

Sheriff Turner shook hands with Kit and thanked her for all her help. Kit felt good about helping the Sheriff; she couldn't believe Debbie was a 'good scent dog' as the Sheriff called her.

Sheriff Turner opened the driver's door. "Kit, you should pursue lessons and certification for Debbie."

She was thinking of the possibility and how that would change their lives as she drove home. It was an honorable profession, but was it in her future?

3

Kit stayed busy getting her house in order for the fall months coming. She had her gutters cleaned, garage cleared out, and trees trimmed, and now she felt it was time to take a road trip.

"Kit, this is Sheriff Houser in Latimer; I'm a couple of hours away from you. I would like to tell you about a situation we have here and present an idea to you."

"Okay, Sheriff, let me get to my office, so I can write notes."

"In this situation, time is ticking away. Lara Mae Underwood, five years old, has wandered away from her home. Her mother said Lara Mae had her puppy with her outside playing. The puppy came back to the house; he was stunned and wobbling around, as if someone had thrown him aside. It is of the essence that we find her now, not later.

This is what I'm putting before you, and I know it's a tough decision, but we need you and your dog—Debbie, right? That's her name? We

27

called Sheriff Turner; he gave me your number. All working dogs are in Dallas helping the Sheriff's Department hunt for a fugitive."

Kit sat there, thoughts zipping through her mind.

Sheriff Houser said, "Miss Carson?"

"Yes, Debbie is her name. I don't know what to say. I know this is as urgent as you say. So, would I leave and come to the Police Department in Latimer?"

"Yes, we will be waiting for you. There are signs when you hit town that will lead you to our office."

Kit didn't understand why she said yes, but something told her she couldn't turn him down. She could not rest until she and Debbie had done their best for the missing child.

*

Thirty minutes had passed since she talked to Sheriff Houser, and she was ready. She had thrown together a small suitcase. She called Clare and said she was heading out of town and would call her as soon as she got back. Debbie seemed to have gotten caught up in the packing frenzy. She jumped around when she saw her favorite toys, the squeaky ball and the stuffed purple frog, in the bag, and her bed loaded in the trunk.

"Okay Debbie, let's go help Lara Mae."

Two hours later, Kit parked in front of the Sheriff's department. She reached under the driver's seat to get Debbie's bowl and water. She drank long and hard. Kit got her out of the car, and they went around the side of the building.

"Okay, Debbie, we can't go far, so do what you need to do." Debbie knew what was expected and got business done.

They walked back around to the front of the Sheriff's Department. She made Debbie sit before they went inside.

"Okay, Debbie, let's go."

Sheriff Houser introduced Kit and Debbie around to each deputy; they let Debbie smell their hands. She wagged her nub, seeming to say, "Hi." She would be out in the field with them, and they wanted her to concentrate on one scent only.

Everyone loaded up and started out. Kit and Debbie piled in the back seat of Deputy Jordan's car. He had too much computer stuff to get in the front.

Deputy Jordan said, "Kit, when we get to the house, Sheriff Houser is going to give you a blouse of Lara Mae's. We will stay back and see if Debbie goes in a direction. Don't feel bad if she doesn't, we thought it might help. There weren't any trained cadaver or scent dogs available."

Kit was shocked to hear the word "cadaver." She wasn't sure how she liked Debbie being known as a cadaver rescue dog. She would think about that later.

They had reached the house; Kit was nervous. The situation was completely out of her range of thinking. She had wanted to get out of town with Debbie for a trip, but this wasn't exactly what she had envisioned.

She and Debbie stood in the front yard. Sheriff Houser said Loren, Lara Mae's mother, had said her ex-husband had called a couple of days ago stating he wanted to take Lara Mae with him. Sheriff Houser brought Lara Mae's blouse.

"Okay Debbie, let's see what will be."

Debbie smelled and looked directly at Kit. They were in the country, and Kit had taken her leash off. Debbie turned and trucked down the winding, dirt road. She put her nose in the air, never looking back or changing directions.

After a while, the Sheriff and his deputies started showing fatigue. They were running and trying to hold everything down on their heavy belts. Debbie suddenly went down a dirt embankment, stopped at a fence line forty feet away, and sat down. It was plain to see a pickup had been parked on the other side of the fence.

"Well, this is where Lara Mae was put in a vehicle," the Sheriff said. "At least we can start looking for a pickup by the tire tracks.

Kit, do you think you can hang around a day? We would put you up at the Upshur Motel in town."

She and Debbie were in a simple, outdated motel room. The decor was like a million others up and down the many highways. Kit remembered the motel rooms she and her family stayed in during vacations. They always rented kitchenettes when they reached their destination. Her favorite had been in Montana, the Roy Roger's furnishings and the plastic table cloth on the chrome-legged kitchen table. She didn't want to, but she had to look at the picture above the bed. Her mother had called it "Motel Art." She looked and chuckled; it was a print of a huge Magnolia flower.

"How perfect."

She dropped Debbie's bed in the big chair; she didn't want the many smells on the carpet to cloud her sense of smell. She didn't have a manual, "How to Track a Smell" by Lord Higgins IV or some other Lord of Fox Tracks.

Debbie seemed a little down, and she didn't want to eat her dinner meal. That made up Kit's mind, then and there; they wouldn't do this again. It wasn't in their plans. Kit wanted to have fun and see the good old US of A. She had no doubt, if someone tried to attack her with Debbie around, it would be bad.

She was feeling guilty about Debbie being so down. She got up, put on her slippers and told

Debbie to get on the bed. It only seemed appropriate for her to sleep at the foot of the bed. Debbie jumped on the bed and went around and around and around some more before lying down in a tight ball. Maybe they would draw strength from each other, waking up in the morning and continuing on to find the child predator.

The next morning she was hanging at the motel. She had already fed Debbie and had a long walk. She was ready to go home, but first things first. Hopefully by tonight she and Debbie would be in their own beds. The Sheriff dropped by her room at 9:00am when he got the call: a baby blanket had been found at Lake Center.

"Let's go see." Sheriff Houser helped get Debbie into the back seat of the Sheriff's patrol car and clicked in.

Lake Center was eight miles from town, and the Sheriff was driving eighty miles an hour. They hit a bump and everyone went to the top of their seat belts. Debbie lay down; Kit put one hand on her back and one on the roof of the patrol car.

The Sheriff looked in his mirror at Kit in the back seat, "Sorry 'bout that."

There were three locals from the Sheriff's Department and two State Trooper patrol cars parked when they drove up.

"Sheriff, we think the ex-husband is still in the area."

"Why would you think that?"

"He had a flat over there and walked away from his pickup. We know the vehicle is registered to him."

They looked where the deputy pointed. A Dodge pickup was parked sideways and the door was left open with a flat on the front left wheel.

Once again the blouse of Lara Mae was brought out for Debbie. Kit took Debbie's leash off. Debbie turned north and took off at a trot. She got away from them and went full speed down the dirt road to the water. They couldn't see Debbie; she was moving fast, but they could see the little whiffs of dirt kicked up by her paws.

They topped the sand berm with Kit in the lead. She was smiling when she looked back at the Sheriff. There was Debbie licking Lara Mae's face at the edge of the water. She had been wandering around by herself close to the water's edge, playing in the sand. They could see by the footprints in the wet sand that someone had walked away.

Lara Mae was taken to the hospital by ambulance to meet her mother. She had been waiting for word at her sister's. The deputies searched the lake around the area and saw where someone had walked to the fence and got in another vehicle.

"Wonder what that was about? Why would he leave Lara Mae there?" Kit asked the Deputy on their way back to the motel.

"We are looking for the ex. We are pretty sure it's him."

Kit commented, "Let's hope it's nothing more devious than a father being stupid because Lara Mae would have been in trouble soon."

4

She and Debbie got home around 7:00pm. Kit was so tired and hungry, but she made sure the alarm was set. She fed Debbie and heated up some soup for herself. That was going to be it for the night. It felt so good to take a shower in her bathroom and climb into her own bed. Debbie had already gotten on her bed and was snoring.

Kit woke up the next morning with the TV still on. She looked around her bedroom and discovered how much she had really missed it while she had been gone that short time. She put on her robe to make coffee and put cinnamon rolls in the oven. Debbie was put out the back. Kit just didn't feel like getting dressed and starting her day.

Clare called to say she woke up with a cold. Kit could tell by her voice.

"I'm just going to take some over-the-counter medicine and see what I feel like in a couple of days."

"Okay, but if you need anything, food, medicine, company, I'm here."

Kit knew Clare would do the same for her. She would call Clare tomorrow to check on her and tell her about what had happened in Latimer.

She remembered the first time they met on the school bus. They had become friends on that very day, and their friendship had endured all these years.

Clare's parents, Mr. and Mrs. Bishop, owned a bait store outside of town. She and Clare usually switched lunches. Kit loved Clare's; they had fried catfish sandwiches with tartar sauce and lettuce. Those were the yummy sandwich fixings that Kit never got in her lunches. Clare loved switching, too, because of the peanut butter, banana, and jelly sandwiches, stuff she never got in hers.

*

Kit was mostly a loner and enjoyed the time she had to herself. How else was a person supposed to get to know themselves or hear that inner voice that tells them everything is ticking along okay or when it's time to get a mole checked out or get that tooth fixed before it went too far?

She couldn't say she didn't have friends because she did. If she needed help, her friends and neighbors would be there, and she felt like she needed to do the same thing for others calling for her help. She had always thought people should care for one another, checking on their neighbors, especially the older ones. Kit talked to all the widowed women and men on her street. If she hadn't seen a neighbor for a couple of days, she would knock on their door. If Kit didn't show up for a couple of days, someone would have come to her door and knocked, too. Every day she and Debbie walked, and she talked to neighbors. It was relaxing and helped her socially, mentally, and physically.

Kit tried to touch base with Clare every couple of days. It had been over a month since Clare had come down with her cold. Her doctor was concerned about her blood pressure and had put her on medication, telling her to take it easy for a while. Kit badly wanted to see Clare, so she gave her a call.

"Clare, how are you doing today?"

"For once I feel like I might be around tomorrow. David is taking me to Casio's Mexican Food Restaurant to eat tonight. Why don't you join us?"

"You know, that sounds wonderful. We haven't seen each other in while, and it will be great to see David."

"We were going about 6 o'clock; is that okay?"

Kit was excited to see her dear friends. "See you there."

The Casio Restaurant smelled delicious and spicy; the noise level was festive and happy. David and Clare were already seated, sharing chips and hot sauce.

"We are having fajitas and a Margarita?"

"Yes and yes again."

They laughed. It had been that kind of week for all three.

David went first, "I went to see a college friend of mine in town. He had gotten a divorce and needed company. We had a great visit."

Next was Clare, "I had Annie put down last week. She had been diagnosed with bladder cancer. I really miss her."

"Clare! Why didn't you call me, I would have been there, you know I would have."

Clare waved it off and picked up a chip, dunking it in the red sauce. Clare told them both she wanted to go out to the Academy and pick a dog. Kit and David thought this was a great idea.

Kit went last, telling them about Debbie helping the Sheriff in Latimer and in Evansville. Both were fascinated and asked a lot of questions.

David asked, "Are you going to continue the rescue project?"

"No, I don't think that's our calling. It took a lot out of Debbie, and I was on edge all the time. I want to have fun with her and get my life back to living a relaxed, joyful retirement." They both smiled, knowing what she meant.

David was four years older than Clare and Kit. When they graduated from high school, David was graduating from the University of Texas. He worked for an Austin technology company for five years. His heart wasn't in the fast-moving city and never-ending traffic. He longed for his hometown and the small-town community feeling. David came home and started his own company building websites. She thought David was handsome and would have gone on a date with him, had he ever asked. The timing over the years had just not been right for the two of them.

During dinner, they laughed and told old, funny stories on one another.

Kit said, "This had been fun and relaxing. I'm glad we did this."

They were ready to go.

Scooting out of the booth, David said, "That was a delicious meal and most enjoyable with the two of you."

At that moment, everything took a turn for the worse. Suddenly, Clare grabbed the front her blouse and had a puzzled look on her face.

"Clare! Clare!" Both were calling her name.

David thought his sister was having a heart attack or a stroke. He took hold of her arms and eased her to a sitting position on the end of the booth. Her eyes rolled back, and she wilted forward. He took control and moved the table up against the other booth. He picked Clare up and laid her flat on the floor. David started CPR while the owner dialed 911.

They followed Clare's gurney out to the ambulance; she hadn't opened her eyes.

Clare was in ER when Kit and David shot through the double doors. They wouldn't know anything for a while the receptionist had told them. Judy Marrow, an RN that she and Clare had gone to school with, came to talk with Kit and David.

"She has a team helping her: doctors, a Respiratory Therapist, and nurses. They will need to look at X-rays, blood work, and, when she's stabilized, she will be transferred to the ICU unit. It's going to be awhile."

They sat in the ER waiting room, staring at the floor, with everyone else waiting for word on their loved ones. This couldn't be happening to Clare; she had to pull through. Clare was strong and loved life; they were meant to have years of fun completing their bucket list together.

Hours later a nurse came to the waiting room and told them to follow her. The nurse stopped in front of Clare's ICU room. The look on her face was enough.

"She is awake, but very weak. You can go in one at a time."

David went first, looking back at Kit with tears in his eyes as he pushed the door open and closed it behind him.

She continuously said prayers for Clare while she paced outside of her room. Clare was the friend that had gone skinny-dipping with her, the friend that got drunk with her the very first time. She walked to the window and leaned against the frame, gazing at the parking lot below. She was seeing the imaginary video in her head like it was yesterday.

Clare and David's parents lived in a two-story house with Clare and David's bedrooms on the second floor. She was spending the night. She and Clare had raided Mr. and Mrs. Bishop's liquor cabinet downstairs. Very quietly they made their way back up the stairs. They started giggling after a couple of sips of something called Cherry Sloe Gin and decided to climb out the second story bedroom window onto the roof. They didn't want to wake Clare's parents.

It's a wonder they hadn't fallen off the roof. David had been home from college over the weekend, and the next day he knew something had happened because they were both throwing up and looked pale. She and Clare were bad together but oh-so-good when it was right.

David came out of Clare's room and said, "She wants to see you."

Kit took a deep breath and walked in. Clare was so pale and looked worn out.

Kit quickly moved to her bed, taking her hand, "Hi, I'm so glad we are sisters, and I can share this with you."

Clare's eyes looked hollowed-out; she looked like she had lost 20 pounds in a matter of hours. Tubes were everywhere with machines monitoring her progress. Kit sat on the bed, then turned and lay close to Clare.

In a weak voice, Clare said, "Kit, you have been my sister, always; I want you to take care of David for me. You have always been the strong one."

"Of course, he's my family too."

Clare's eyes fluttered and closed. The nurse's station alarms were going off. A 'code blue' was in effect, and Kit was rushed out of the room. She and David were there waiting for news they knew was coming. The doctor came out of the room thirty minutes later.

He came directly to them and said he was sorry. "Her heart was weakened by the respiratory infection."

The nurse said they were allowed back in the room to pay their respects. Kit looked at her childhood friend; she was glad they had met each other and shared so many precious times together. David and Kit held each other close, sobbing beside Clare's hospital bed.

5

Clare's will stated she wanted a graveside service with all pets in attendance with their owners. David had published in the local newspaper that the graveside service would be Saturday 10 o'clock, at the Evansville Cemetery.

David and Bishoff were standing by the casket that would be lowered later. Bishoff had a black scarf tied around his neck and looked so regal sitting beside David. Clare and David's cousins were there and had brought their pets. One cousin had brought her cat in a carrier with a black scarf tied around the handle. People were there from town; Clare had touched many lives while on earth. Kit and Debbie stood among Clare's friends to give their final respects.

After the service, Kit took Debbie home and gave her water and fed her. They took a walk through the neighborhood, and she cried with the widow women for all they had lost in the past, too. Mrs. Prater had lost her husband (sixty-four) and son (thirty-three) in an automobile accident two years before. That had to be harder than losing Clare, but at that moment she didn't know how. She was sure what the widow women said is true: "It never goes away, but it eases with time." She didn't like the other saying: "Time heals all." Kit knew no amount of time would heal this.

Kit rested on her bed and didn't feel like eating or watching TV. Nothing was going to be the same again. She wasn't prepared for Clare to be here one moment then gone the next. Kit and David's lives had changed forever in that moment.

Debbie knew something was wrong; she knew her master needed her. Quietly, she jumped up on the bed and dropped next to Kit, licking her hand. Kit was glad for the company and kisses. She knew in the deepest place of her heart that Clare was gone and in a better place. It wasn't time for the three of them to become two, but it was true...

A black cloud hovered over the week, and she couldn't make it go away. Kit wanted to leave town for a couple of days, take Debbie somewhere, shop, eat out, and not think about all this.

The days were long; time seemed to stand still, and Kit didn't have the energy to go or do anything. At times in her mind, it seemed like the black cloud would close in over her.

Two more days until Clare's will would be read in the offices of Ledger, Smith and Blackburn, Attorneys-At-Law. She and David would be the only ones there; no one else was mentioned in her will. It was to be the finality of Clare's life wishes. After that, Kit had to put one foot in front the other; no longer would she hear her dear old friend's voice of wisdom, clarity, and humor.

*

Mr. Blackburn led her down a hall to his office where David was waiting. Mr. Blackburn started off by saying Clare had come to his office a week before her death, after her cat died. She wanted to make sure her wishes were met.

Kit was astonished that Clare had done that so recently. Did she have a premonition of all to come? She couldn't concentrate on what Mr. Blackburn was saying.

"To David I leave my house, furnishings, stocks, bonds and cars. He doesn't need the money, so I leave all the money to Kit. Do wonderful things with it, Kit. Have fun, dream big, and I will be waiting for you both someday."

"What? What did you say? Why would she do that?"

"It's all very legal, Kit," Mr. Blackburn said. "Those were her wishes. She told me you wouldn't want the inheritance, but to make you understand how much she loved you and that this is what she wanted."

Mr. Blackburn gave David a piece of paper with the total amount of the estate. He gave a piece of paper to Kit with her amount.

"David, do you know how much money this is?" She had a shocked look on her face.

"Yes, Kit, I have my own money. She knew this, so don't think it's unfair to me, okay?"

"I will have to think on this tonight." She was dumbfounded and didn't know what else to say.

Mr. Blackburn said, "It will take about a month to get everything ready, and then I will call you both."

Kit and David walked out together. David said, "Do you want to go somewhere and talk about this over a drink or lunch?"

"Yes, I'm overwhelmed right now."

"Let's go to the Courthouse Cafe. Will you follow me, or do you want me to drive?"

"I will meet you there. I have to stop and buy some treats for Debbie at the Dog Academy store."

"Okay Kit, see you there."

She was lost at the Academy store and kept thinking about the last time she and Clare had been there. She thought she was going to cry, so she grabbed Debbie's Buffalo treats, paid for them, and hurried to her car. She sat in her car bawling, grieving for her dear friend; it seemed she had lost a part of herself, too.

David saw the worried look on Kit's face as he got up to meet her. They hugged and sat down.

David said first, "I knew she was going to do this, and I begged her to tell you about it. But she said, 'Maybe Kit will go first and all these plans will have to be changed again.' First, she loved you like a real sister; second of all, she knew you would always be there for her. If I was the one to go first, you would have been there for her, all the way. So here you are going through this with me."

That made Kit cry. Reaching in her purse and bringing out a Kleenex, she said, "Let's order a Margarita."

They talked about the experiences the three of them had together in the span of the years. They made a toast, "Clare's gentle soul will be missed terribly, but never forgotten."

"David, I'm going to take a trip with Debbie. I don't know where, but when I do I'll call you. You and I are still buds forever, right? I will call you before I go. We have a while before we go back to the law office."

"That sounds like a great idea, and when you get back I may have you keep Bishoff while I take some time off."

"You got it."

*

Kit was packing suitcases. She wanted to get in her car and go, period. She didn't care if it was Montana, Dallas, Colorado or Timbuktu, Africa. She remembered her father saying, "We're going to Ten-buck-two," when they were going someplace far away, usually fishing.

She needed a change of scenery and to talk to people who were happy and positive. Kit was hoping she could draw strength and direction from others.

She put four folded pieces of paper in a bowl. On each piece of paper was a letter: N, S, E, W. She pulled out a piece of paper and unfolded it to reveal the "N." Now she knew she was going north. Later tonight she would decide which way north.

The next morning, before she put Debbie in the car, she called David. She got his answering machine.

"Hi David, I'm taking off this morning to the wild and unknown. I will call you later and let you know where we are. Oh yeah, please drive by my house every once in a while. You have my cell number."

Debbie's seatbelt was buckled; she was super excited and panting in the back seat, drooling all over the towel Kit had placed over the seat. The luggage was in the trunk, and they were pulling out of the driveway. She couldn't say when she would be back and maybe only then to pack and move somewhere else.

Today her route was to get to Abilene, Texas to the KOA campgrounds. The website looked okay to spend their first night on the road, and they had a dog park. How great was that? She had called this morning and reserved a one-bedroom cabin for the night and promised the managers she would not leave Debbie alone at the campgrounds.

Tonight in Abilene would be a nightgown and snacks night. This is what she needed, relaxation and to slow down with nothing on her mind but having fun and looking around. With all that in mind, she hoped a life-plan would materialize.

Deciding what she wanted to do for the rest of her life was a big enchilada on her plate and, at the moment, she didn't have a clue. She and Debbie checked in the KOA in Abilene. They walked the grounds to get exercise and got settled for the night. She had one more night on the road and had made a reservation at the KOA in Lubbock, and then she thought she could make it to Ruidoso, New Mexico, the next. Kit had never been to Ruidoso. She had always wanted to go. She started singing a song from her teen years, "Happiness was Lubbock, Texas in My Rear View Mirror" by Mack Davis. Debbie howled along with Kit. They traveled most of the day, stopping and taking water and bathroom breaks at their leisure.

Kit looked at the scenery out her front windshield, then at Debbie in the rearview mirror. Kit had rolled down Debbie's window. She was taking in all the smells of traveling down the road with the wind in her face.

She was tired today and although it was only two and half more hours to Lubbock, she wanted to figure out the lay of the land, where she was going to walk Debbie, and get settled in their cabin. By three o'clock, she and Debbie were in Lubbock. She got off the interstate and found a local drive-in and hang-out. She ordered a hamburger for Debbie and a cheeseburger for herself. Getting Debbie out of the car was next; walking her around got the attention of several people eating in their cars. Debbie was beautiful, and as if she knew people were talking about her, she kept her head high and padded around like a panther, plopping down her big paws.

They were twenty minutes from the Lubbock KOA she had reserved for the night.

Kit checked in with Debbie by her side, sitting quietly. The manager was impressed, as she knew he would be. The small cabin was like the one in Abilene and was what she was looking for tonight. She took Debbie to the dog park on the grounds. Next, they went to the restroom and shower onsite. Kit locked the door and quickly washed the day off.

Thirty minutes later, she was opening her cooler and singing another song by a Lubbock singer, Buddy Holly. "That will be the day..." She had to quit after a couple of bars because Debbie thought this was another sing along.

Kit had a case of Buffalo canned dog food in her trunk and had brought in two cans. She had done this in case she couldn't find a place to stop and eat. This was one of those nights: "Debbie, please accept this food for the night." Debbie didn't care; she was content to be with her master. Kit opened her cooler and got a beer, peanuts, chips and chicken jerky out to drink, eat, and be merry. She turned on the TV for the weather report; tomorrow was going to be breezy and a great day to travel. She turned off the TV; she just wasn't into TV on this trip.

Debbie was on her bed snoring, and Kit let her mind wander. What was she going to do? She had her support system in Evansville with friends, but was that enough now? She wanted to meet new friends, go to different places and start a new life. Would she always be afraid to move out of her comfort zone? Ruidoso was tomorrow and a new town to explore.

6

Kit drove into Ruidoso Valley on Thursday afternoon about 3 o'clock. The sunlight was fading fast behind a mountain. She stopped at the Chamber of Commerce on the main square, and took Debbie in the office with her. Lola, the Chamber of Commerce office manager, told her they were starting the Aspen Fest that weekend. The parade Saturday started at the top of the hill at 10:00am. Today the booths were being assembled and people were allowed to set up for Friday, the beginning of the festival. There would be an Arts and Crafts show, a Chili Cook Off, and the Hot Rod Run and Car Show. The Chamber of Commerce was the host each year, Lola told her. She would be able to take Debbie everywhere she went. Kit inquired about cabins to rent for a week.

Lola asked her if she wanted to stay in town or be out a little ways. Kit said close to town for the first week. Why did she say that? She didn't even know if she wanted to stay a whole week.

Lola told her that there weren't many cabins left because of the Aspen Fest. She had a one bedroom, one bath condo, and Debbie would be welcome. Someone had called that morning canceling their reservations for the week.

Kit told Lola, "I won't leave Debbie alone in the condo. I will take her with me."

Lola said, "Okay, the Siena condo will be it."

They both agreed Kit should come back in the office after the week and make reservations for an extended visit if she wanted to stay. Kit asked if she would be close to the river.

"Yes, and the kitchen is stocked with snacks and the linens are provided." Kit just needed to check off the list of food she ate.

Lola gave her the keys and took Kit's credit card number for the deposit. "Have fun! I will see you in a week, if not sooner at the events tomorrow."

The condo was on the main road going through town, and she could walk with Debbie to all the festivities. She didn't want to stop anywhere this afternoon and planned on giving Debbie a couple of cans of dog food. She would raid the stocked kitchen and see what was there before going to the grocery store tomorrow. The condo was backed up to the crystal clear Ruidoso River that snaked through town. She opened the back sliding glass doors and took a big breath while listening to the river rushing along.

"Wow, Debbie, it smells so clean. Someone is fixing bar-b-que, and I'm hungry, aren't you?" Debbie marched with her paws up and down.

The condo was equipped with a gas fireplace. Kit pushed a button on the wall and, voilà, fire leapt-up on the blue glass pieces across the bottom. Debbie jumped sideways, and then charged to the hearth barking.

"No Debbie, it's okay. It's just heat, not an intruder." Debbie wasn't sure. Kit laughed and said to her, "We haven't had cold enough weather to start the fireplace in Texas."

While Debbie ate her dog food, Kit took peanut butter crackers and potato chips out of the basket on the table. She took a Dr. Pepper out of the refrigerator, checking the items off the list. She was glad she had brought her and Debbie's suitcases in and locked the car before relaxing because it was cold and dark outside. She wasn't used to this; Texas sunsets were for-e-v-e-r.

Now the whole day was behind her, Kit turned on the TV in the bedroom and found a local channel for the weather tomorrow. It was supposed to be a cool thirty-eight degrees but clear. In the bathroom, Kit found a button to push on the edge of the tub and a perfect stream of water came out of the ceiling, filling the soaking tub. Debbie had followed her into the bathroom and was looking at the water coming out of the ceiling. She turned around and went back to her bed.

"How lush is this?" She was in the soaking tub with a thick bubble bath surrounding her. Could she live in a town like this? Would she and Debbie like tromping around in the snow a good part of each year? How would she feel about not being close to her friends in Evansville? Would they come to visit her in Ruidoso? She wanted to talk to David and see what was happening at home. She climbed out of the tub and dried off, putting on her favorite old flannel gown that had been washed so many times it was super soft. She dug out just what she needed, a Victoria Secret robe she had bought a gazillion years ago. It was pink candy-stripped, long, billowing and super comfy. She smelled the robe, and it brought back the smell of home.

She laughed to herself, "That's what I needed for tonight. I know I still have a home in Texas."

*

"Kit, I was just thinking about you. How's everything there?"

"David, there's a festival going on in town this weekend. Debbie can go everywhere with me."

He sounded down. "Nothing's happening here. I drove by your house yesterday, and it looks well-kept. I don't think you will have any problems. Your neighbors saw me passing and waved. They, too, are watching the house for you.”

“God bless their souls; there is a special place in heaven for those that help others. I have a question for you. If I bought a house or condo here, would you come and visit?”

“Hmm, I like Ruidoso and so did Clare. A friend in high school used to take us with his family snow skiing in Ruidoso every once in a while. Are you thinking about taking up residence there?” She could hear the panic in his voice.

“I don’t know yet. I would like a place to go to for the summer, but I’m not sure if I want to live here permanently. I do like the Texas sunshine. It’s something to think about; at least I would have some culture in my life. I’m going to be here a week, as I rented a condo, and hopefully by then I will know where I want to go from here.

I feel like I’m supposed to be doing something with my life. I dreamt last night I had an animal adoption agency for senior and elderly people, partnered with older dogs. An agency that catered to seniors and animals alike, placing the perfect older match together. Debbie is six years old, and she still has a wonderful life to live with an older person, me. But I see myself still in Texas starting a business, not here.”

“Yes, I do feel sometimes that I’ve wasted my life. I could have had a family. I have the money, so that wasn’t the reason. Now that Clare is gone,

I can't face the reality of truly being alone. I was never lonely with Clare around."

Kit replied, "We both need something to bring us out of this slump. Clare wouldn't want us to do this to ourselves. Remember, she said, 'Live like there's no tomorrow.' So why don't you come here to Ruidoso and join me? Bring Bishoff with you; he would love it with us on an adventure." She waited to see what he would say.

"I-I think I will. I need the road trip with Bishoff, and you are right that he would love it. Thank you, Kit, I'm already excited. I will start packing as soon as we get off the phone."

"Wonderful, tomorrow is Friday. We can go see Lola Monday and see if anything else is available. I will also see if I can't find an adventure for us to take with the dogs. How does that sound?"

"I will be on the way by 5 o'clock in the morning. Kit, this is exciting, and Bishoff doesn't know what's happening, but he's wagging his tail and turning in circles. I will call you tomorrow night, probably in Abilene. It just depends on traffic and Bishoff needing to stop, but we're coming. Thank you, Kit, I think this is just what we needed."

Kit told him, "Make a reservation at the KOA in Abilene and Lubbock. It's what you and Bishoff need for the night. They have a dog park and showers."

*

She and Debbie left the condo to walk Friday morning. She wanted to see the town and talk to the people that lived here all the time, not just the weekenders. That was the only way to find out if she really wanted to live in Ruidoso or the area.

The first person she saw was Lola. Lola introduced her to Gary Andrews, the event carpenter, and John and Judy Walker. John was the auctioneer for the prizes at the end of Saturday's events. All the money would be donated to a charity. Judy, his wife, had a booth of preserves and salsas. Kit picked out six of each: peach, jalapeño, blueberry jam and fresh, corn relish and hot salsa. They could be Xmas presents, or she and David could consume them all. She paid and told Judy she would be back to pick up her purchases. Debbie was excited, smelling each of the other dogs as they passed by.

They had a log splitting contest, a Punch and Judy show for the kids, and all kinds of wooden bear figurines, from table-sized to life-sized yard art. Kit walked past a booth setting up for homemade dog treats. Debbie got double treats from Janet Wernicke, the lady baker. Kit bought peanut butter flavored nuggets, smothered steak and gravy flavored biscuits, and organic orange oatmeal cookies for Debbie's dessert. She and David might need these to entice the dogs.

At the local meat market on the drag, she stopped and asked a gentleman in a blue apron sitting on a bench in front of the store watching the excitement, "Sir, I know you work here, and I would like to buy one Porter House steak and a baking potato. I'm respectful of the market and didn't want to bring Debbie in, but I can't leave her outside either."

The owner, Andy Lyles, said he didn't mind at all; he thought Debbie was gorgeous. He had raised Rotts when he was younger and every once in a while someone would bring by an older Rott he had sold them as a pup from his sire. She and Andy sat on the bench and exchanged Rott tales. Kit explained how she had gotten Debbie and the adventures and journeys they had already been on together.

Andy left her sitting on the bench to check off the list Kit had given him. She would have to make two stops along the way to collect the other purchases from the vendors. Andy said he could help and gave them a ride on his ATV. They stopped and gathered the preserves, dog treats and a bottle of local wine. Debbie was patiently waiting in the ATV, but she watched intently, never letting Kit out of her sight.

Andy helped her bring all her goodies in the kitchen and left. She said he would be seeing her again tomorrow. Debbie was thirsty and hungry;

she could smell the dog treats and was continuously circling the table where Kit had laid them. Kit gave Debbie her canned Buffalo dog food, thinking she would have to buy dry dog food tomorrow or maybe David would bring a large bag, but she decided for the time being it was a good stand-by. Debbie was going to get an organic oatmeal cookie for dessert.

"Sit Debbie, please." Debbie sat and was prancing on her front feet for her treat. "Okay, you big ham."

She got the potato ready for the oven. She didn't like microwaved potatoes; the texture wasn't right. She opened the bottle of rich red wine from Ruidoso Valley Vineyards to go with the steak. Thank goodness there was a down-draft gas grill on the stove. She lit the candle in the middle of the table and poured herself a goblet of wine. Debbie decided the fireplace wasn't such a bad thing. Every time she laid down in the living room, she got a little closer on the rug to the fireplace and heat.

The meal was fabulous, and she had a healthy appetite for a change.

"Does food always taste better in the mountains, Debbie?"

She blamed it on the mountains, the altitude and attitude. She took her wine to the front porch. Kit sat on the steps, sipping her wine, and Debbie sat beside her, always vigilant.

Kit was watching people walk by with smiles and laughter in their voices. She was thinking about Clare.

She said softly to the big moon, "I so wish you were here, Clare." She had heard the sadness in David's voice too.

7

She had slept until 9 o'clock. That was unusual for her. Debbie was still on her bed sleeping, as if she knew they would be there for a while, and it was okay for her to sleep in. It was Saturday; Kit threw on a comfortable pair of jeans, sweat shirt, her winter angora socks, leather boots and the only heavy coat she owned.

She and Debbie walked to the creek while waiting for the coffee maker to finish brewing. Debbie waded out in the creek to drink water. Her head came up fast; she was looking at a deer across the water in a thicket. Kit didn't say anything, as she was afraid Debbie would take off after the deer. Debbie stared a moment longer and turned to go back to the condo.

"Whew, Debbie, that took a load off my mind."

David had called while she was outside. He had left a message saying he was on the road and should be there by Sunday afternoon. She could hear Bishoff breathing close to the cell phone.

She was excited about them coming and would have everything ready when they arrived.

That night Kit was sitting on the couch making lists for the next day. She glanced at the flames in the fireplace, wondering, "Could I be romantically involved with David?"

She laughed and said, "I don't know, the situation hasn't presented itself."

She felt they both needed friendship right now: a soft, emotional, platonic connection to bring back the secure feeling they both needed to move on. She would have to wait and see.

"You never know," she laughed again, saying to Debbie. "You just never know."

That morning, she and Debbie walked to Andy's, taking in all the laughter and excitement from the festival along the way. Kit poked her head in the door and asked if Andy was available.

The clerk held up one finger, "Just a moment."

Andy came out within a couple of minutes, sitting on the bench with her.

She made small talk, "Andy, if you could live here in the summer and go somewhere else for the winter, would you?"

"Hummm, I have lived here for the past twenty-one years. It's cold here in the winter, and my arthritis gives me plenty of trouble. My wife complains about the snow, her cold bones, and cabin fever. So, yes, if it wasn't for my livelihood, I would not just spend the winters somewhere else, I would move somewhere else period, forever and ever. Why? Are you thinking of relocating here?"

"It's crossed my mind. I just lost a dear, lifelong friend and feel adrift. I thought maybe a move would help me alleviate the loneliness, try meeting new people, but I'm not sure. I don't want to add more problems for myself and never feel grounded."

Andy looked at her, and then looked down at the ground.

"Kit...I have learned over the years that neither a place nor a person can make you happy; you have to do that within yourself, or you will be continuously looking for something or someone and maybe never find it. There's a saying, 'If you can't love the one you want-then love the one you're with.' I think that goes for places too."

*

The Aspen festival was still going strong and an Indian flat bread taco truck was across from her condo. She walked across the highway to get tacos. She put the three tacos in her bag from Andy's; hurrying back across the street to eat by the fireplace. She ate one taco and gave the other two to Debbie.

She made a cup of hot chocolate, curling up on the couch, thinking she would take a soaking tub bath tonight while she had the time before David showed up.

As she watched the flames in the fireplace again, her thoughts were about the here, the now, and the future. She made one decision. She didn't want to live where her bones, hands and feet were cold seven or eight months out of the year. She liked the gentle warming sun shining on her face as the Texas mornings got warmer. There weren't that many bone-cold days during the winter months in Texas.

Thinking out loud, "I don't own a full season of winter clothes. I own one heavy coat, a few sweaters, jeans, and I brought those with me."

*

During the 'dog days of summer' she wanted to get away from the Texas-hot summer days and nights. Maybe she could lease a condo in Colorado or go to Wyoming for the dry, hot summer months. She wouldn't have to pay property taxes or worry about having a second house. She wouldn't have a call in the middle of the night, "Kit, there's water running out your front door." She wouldn't have to hurry back to Ruidoso to clean up and restore what had flooded from a frozen, broken pipe or the many other things that could go wrong. Besides, she didn't snow ski, race horses, or ride a motorcycle, and those were the main attractions in Ruidoso.

She felt a little bit better, deciding not to buy a piece of property, but to rent for a couple of months in the summer where it was cool. She saw the need to downsize, not buy more furniture, dishes and linens; less was better now that she was aging. One decision down! This trip away from home had given her a different perspective about her life.

*

It was Sunday. David and Bishoff would be there later in the day. The Aspen festival ended the day before; she had enjoyed watching the excitement from her front porch. She didn't feel like participating or walking through the crowds of people anymore. She felt someone had taken a knife and hollowed-out her core being.

"Will I ever get over this?"

The roast was in the oven. In a couple of hours she would pull the pork roast out, cut up the roasted potatoes, then put everything back in the oven to warm for later. Next, she washed the locally-grown Evansville pinto beans she had soaked overnight in the refrigerator. Miss Rose, her neighbor, gave them to her when she heard about the trip.

She would simmer them all day. Her Granny Carson had taught her how to cook pinto beans with a quirk; Granny put the morning's leftover coffee in the bean water to cook. She had always liked the smoky flavor it gave the beans. Kit stayed busy tidying the condo and walking Debbie along the creek.

She cleaned the bathroom since they would be sharing. She packed all her toiletries and put them in her closet. Kit was taking the extra blanket, sheets and pillow from the top shelf when she turned and saw Debbie in the closet with her.

"It's okay Debbie. I won't leave without you."

She heard knocking on the door about four o'clock. Debbie smelled Bishoff and started barking.

"Shoo, shoo," Kit said, opening the door. "Come in. Hi, Bishoff. David, let me give you a big welcome hug."

Kit helped David bring in all his stuff, including Bishoff's bed and toys.

"I'm so glad you are here. Now we can decide what the heck we are going to do with ourselves." They put David's suitcase in the coat closet and straightened the condo. "Let's feed the dogs and take a short walk along the creek. Later, we can take them again to the creek's edge for their last bathroom trip."

David was used to his mother and Clare telling him what should be done. Clare had been a bossy sister until he got his own place. Now, he most definitely wished Clare were here to do just that, but Kit handled it fine. Later that night would be soon enough for him to put his two cents worth in the conversation, but for now he would just go along.

Bishoff and Debbie were right in tune with each other. Kit and David didn't have to holler or yank on their collars; the dogs were trained "to be in the moment and function as a pack." They made the brisk walk while stopping and looking at all the twinkling stars in the sky. They seemed so close compared to the Texas skies.

"I remember now, the stars always looked bigger and closer here." David was thinking about Clare and the fun times they used to have coming here.

Kit saw his face turn serious; she put her hand on his, hoping this would give him strength as they hurried back to the condo for warmth.

David said, "Something smells wonderful; you cooked in today?"

"Yes, I went to the grocery store and bought a small roast for pulled-pork and potato. The hot sauce and homemade tortillas on the table are from the festival."

She handed David the wine and opener. They were both nervous and maybe this would break the surface while they waited for the food to warm.

"You took off so fast from Evansville; I thought maybe something was wrong?"

Kit took a sip of wine, "I couldn't handle walking around my house all day and thinking about Clare and the wonderful, funny times we had together. Everywhere I went people were talking about Clare. I needed a change; it looks like this trip has been good for you, too, a change of scenery."

"Thank you for inviting us. I think this is the first trip Bishoff has been on. He loved it. I would roll down the window in each town so he could smell and look around while we were slowly passing through. He stayed right with me when we got out of the car. I guess he thought I might leave him someplace. It's amazing in such a short time how we have become attached to each other."

They returned to the couch. "I like this condo, Kit." David walked to the fireplace and pushed the button. W-h-o-o-s-h. Debbie and Bishoff jumped and barked. Kit laughed, telling him about Debbie's first time.

"There are other places to rent now that the festival is over."

"No, this couch is comfy, and I don't want to load everything up again."

"Alright, it's decided."

"Okay, I guess I can start by telling you what's been going on at home. I called the Salvation Army to come to Clare's house and pick up bagged clothes and shoes. I haven't finished going through all the closets; I got so depressed I couldn't finish. How do family members get through this process of clearing their loved one's home? I still have her garage to clean out. You know she had a potter's wheel and gave lessons up until a few years ago. Do you remember that?"

"Yes, I wasn't talented enough to dabble in it, but I did buy, or should I say Clare gave me, a vase that is gorgeous with blue and green hues. How did she make all the money she gave to me? It wasn't all from your parents' estate, was it?"

"In the beginning, it was the small inheritance from our parents that started us investing. We lucked out when we hired a good financial adviser to help us plan for the future. He helped us stay on the right track throughout our lives. Our first cousin June, you remember her, has the keys to Clare's house and is finishing the closets while I'm gone. I told her to take anything that she might use. I need to finish cleaning out the house and put it on the market."

"I forgot about Clare's things. I know what it was like for me when my parents died, and I was left by myself to clean out our house. It was devastating. I can help you when we get back. We will tackle it together. I will leave when you do. That way we can follow each other back."

"Thank you, Kit, for everything."

They both stood and walked to the kitchen to fill their glasses again and break the solemn mood.

Kit was leaning against the counter, "I guess I can go next. The three of us have known each other since grade school and this has been an overwhelming emotional experience for both of us. We never think this time will come; we think it will never happen to us. You know I added you in my will in case something happens to me."

"Yes, I did you, too; you are the only one I truly trust. You have never done any wrong or meanness to me or Clare."

"Thank you, David, same here." They returned to the warm security of the fire.

David went on, "Clare knew how to finish my sentences for me. We had been like that since we were kids. We only wanted the best for each other. I have tried to reach down in myself and grab hold, to get a grip, but I just can't get a handle on this. The intensity of the situation has been overwhelming. I think I've been in shock for a while. I was supposed to go first, not Clare." David gulped and big tears started down his cheek. Kit leaned over and gave him a big hug and he hugged her back.

"I know, David, this is so hard. What do we do now? Where and how do we move forward? I know we are going to have to have a strategy if we are to survive and move on. It's that 'faith-not-fear' thing Wes Moore, the motivator, talks about."

"Kit, maybe we should get some kind of business going, like the one you dreamed. I was thinking on the long stretches of monotonous Texas highways: what if we had an intermediate place for the trained dogs from the dog academy, a place for the younger and older dogs to stay and keep their training up-to-date until they were adopted? It would be a place where they wouldn't lose everything they have learned by going back to a shelter once the trainer has graduated. We would have an arrangement with different shelters and rescue organizations for their animals to come to our facility, and they would get the adoption fee once they are adopted."

Kit had thought about the dream; it kept popping into her mind. She was on a roll now, too, picking up the conversation, "It's such a waste. Debbie is an older dog and a lot of families want a younger dog, but for the older folks like us, it's perfect. We could buy some acreage and build dog cages, training grounds, and a swimming pool—something like the Dog Academy in our area."

"Kit, I like the idea."

They both decided it was time to eat. It had been a long day for David.

"Let's sleep on the idea and see what we can come up with in the morning over coffee."

Bishoff and Debbie were asleep by the fireplace, tired and contented. They didn't care if dinner was served.

The pulled pork tacos were exactly what they needed. They finished and made up David's bed on the couch. They put on their coats and scarfs to make the last run with the dogs.

*

The next morning they tried to stay out of each other's space. Kit got dressed and made her bed.

She joined David in the kitchen. "Hope you had a restful night?"

He looked confused about what to do next, so Kit said, "I'm through in the bathroom. Why don't you take your chance and go for it? I will make breakfast, and then we can discuss our plans and goals over coffee. Agreed?"

Kit fixed bacon and eggs with French toast. She fed the dogs and put the meal in the oven on low to stay warm. This was their unfamiliar adult relationship of "getting to know you" without Clare to fill in the blanks. They had been friends forever, but she knew their relationship had changed for her when he walked in the Condo.

They hooked up the dogs when David came out, and then took a quick walk to the river's edge.

David said as they walked, "I saw your light on at 5 o'clock this morning. I had been up since 3 o'clock drawing plans for the compound." It was nervous chatter between them. "Let's take a look while we eat."

David brought out his drawing while Kit placed the warm breakfast on the table.

"This is what I put on paper."

He had drawn out how he thought the compound should be set up. Kit asked about the small buildings.

Proud of his design, David said, "We have the pool and maintenance facility, and here's where I think the training center or gym should be located. Over here, at the back of the compound, are the agility runs, walking paths, and small gated sections for individual training. What do you think?"

"I think it's wonderful. This may be what we need to help us get over this hurdle and be productive."

They sat at the table eating with gusto while ironing out the wrinkles. Kit was proud of their ideas, and she knew she could trust David as a partner. She got another piece of paper and wrote down the minor adjustments and new ideas with one hand while she crunched on a piece of bacon in the other.

Noontime they decided to walk to Andy's. They had decided to cook spaghetti. That way they could cook and simmer the pasta while they talked about a name for the academy, what part of town would be the best location, and what part Kit and David would play in the organization. They also needed to talk about a facility for all their products and an office area, not to mention hiring trainers and a veterinary service. The list grew and grew.

75

8

Andy Lyles gave David a warm-hearted handshake. He took their shopping list and left them to sit outside with Debbie and Bishoff.

David said, "Very nice gentleman, Andy."

"Yes, he's like a big teddy bear and likes big dogs. He used to raise Rotts."

While they were waiting for Andy to bring their purchases, they continued throwing out ideas, "We could name it the 'In-Between Dog Academy?"

Kit said, "I actually like the title."

David said, "The Younger and Senior Dog Academy."

Kit said, "Too long, let's just keep brain storming."

They discussed taking the 6-years-plus dogs from the shelters, and training them for the purpose of companionship with seniors. If the older dog out-lasted the person, they would take the dog back and match them with another senior. No euthanizing. They discussed a facility for the dogs that were sick and under a veterinarian's care, and a complete daycare facility for the elderly dogs.

Andy returned with the groceries and sat at the end of the bench with them.

David jumped in first. "We would like to throw out an idea and see what you think. We know this idea is not new and it's being done by other people and organizations, but not in our area."

Andy was intrigued. "Shoot."

Kit took the lead. "We want to start an academy for older dogs and match them with senior citizens. A lot of older people are intimidated by younger dogs. They don't have the energy or the patience it takes to train a younger dog. Our idea would allow seniors to adopt an older dog that suits their purpose, a trained dog companion that gives the senior peace of mind when they go to sleep. We would also take the younger dogs that weren't adopted and who would be going back to a shelter after their trainer graduated. They would learn new duties, and some would be trained to become better at a purpose. We would make a website with key words, making it easy to find us. So, what do you think, Andy?"

Andy had a smile on his face. "I think that's a wonderful idea. There is a place in time when a person needs to be comforted by an animal in their home, and there are plenty of dogs that would appreciate having a person that shows them affection and love. It's a win-win situation."

Andy said he had put two large bones in the paper bag and waved them away when they tried to pay.

They were ready and excited to get back home and start on their project. David called a friend of his in real estate. When they got back, the agent would have several investment properties for them see.

*

They both felt elated about their idea and, for the first time, grounded and connected with that little voice inside again, the one that said, "I'm moving in a positive way." They cooked, drew more plans on paper, and twice a day took a break and walked to a nearby park to exercise the dogs. David would take a ball and make Bishoff stay while he threw the ball for Debbie and vice versa. They didn't talk much during this time but concentrated on being assertive, learning from each other, and laughing a lot.

They walked the dogs in town, stopping at different stores, buying trinkets to take back home. One would have to stay outside while the other went in the store. They wanted to try leaving the dogs outside while they went inside. They both walked their dog in a circle and then placed them side by side with their backs to the wall. Both gave the command to stay, and then dropped their leashes.

They went inside and watched out the front store windows. Debbie and Bishoff lay down and kept watch for them coming out the door.

The store owner was looking over their shoulders. "What's going on?"

Kit explained they were training their pets to stay outside and wait for them.

*

They were sitting on the couch waiting for the other one to begin the conversation.

David turned sideways on the couch and looked at Kit. "We have known each other most of our lives. I trust you and feel we would make good business partners. This idea would make a difference in animals and people's lives. It would give us a purpose, to safeguard what these animals have learned and match them with a person of need."

Kit was lost in her own thoughts. "I remember a dog I saw at the Highway 71 pull-off rest area between Marble Falls and Llano years ago. I had been traveling to San Angelo and pulled into the rest area to get water out of the back of my car. As I was bringing the water out of my cooler, I saw him there at the edge of a tree line. I called to him, 'Hi, pup. Come here and I will give you some water.' I wanted to take the dog with me, but I was traveling. I left some water in a plastic bowl and a sandwich. He wouldn't come to me, but if I had taken a little bit more time..."

She stood, still talking as she walked to the fireplace to turn up the flame, "I can still see that cute dog in my mind, even though it's been years. I always wanted to know if someone stopped, took the time, and eventually took him home. I would like to think they did. That's what I want to happen with our academy. We are going to take the time and take that dog home."

She needed to purge as much as David. "I have always had a pet companion as far back as I can remember. My mother told me, 'Kit, if you are going to have a pet, then it will be your responsibility.' Missy, the dachshund, was my first childhood dog. Do you remember Missy? She was my best friend and she listened to every sentence I said, especially the ones that mentioned treats. I came home to feed, water, and walk her every day after school. She was my responsibility."

David laughed, "Yes, I remember Missy. Her belly nearly touched the ground. She was always glad to see me when I came with Clare to pick you up." David picked up the conversation, "Our parents wouldn't let us have pets, so I guess that's why Clare and I have always had a pet companion after we moved away from home."

They were both in their own thoughts. Kit looked David straight in the eyes, "I know Clare would want us to go on. We both have to turn and start walking the other way for our lives to become productive and healthy again. One door closes and another one opens."

"I know we do, Kit, and at least this grieving that comes over me without warning isn't every single moment anymore." He took a breath, "I loved my sister and that comfortable relationship we had with each other. No matter how much time had passed, the conversation picked up where we left off. There's a large, burning hole in my heart. I feel my heart has literally broken into pieces. My immediate family is gone, except you, Kit. You were always that constant in Clare's and my life. Even though there were periods of time that we didn't see each other, Kit, I always knew you and Clare were there for me."

Kit replied, "Remember when you and I hugged throughout our lives? I always put my head on your chest where your heart is. I've always thought you had a strong, loud heartbeat."

9

They were leaving in the morning and following each other back home. They had made reservations at the same KOAs as on the way up. In the evenings after driving all day, they could brainstorm on the ideas that came to mind during the vast spaces of Texas prairie land.

They took the dogs and made their way around town to say their goodbyes. Lola at the Chamber of Commerce was first. Kit turned in her key and the list of supplies used. David tried to pay the bill, but Kit wasn't having it. They walked to Andy's grocery store next and hugged the big butcher. He in return wished them well in their endeavor with the Dog Academy. It had been a wonderful trip; they both had a direction to go and a worthy cause to help them with the healing process.

Kit turned to David after they had loaded the luggage and dogs. "This is going to be so much fun and I think Clare would approve of our idea and partnership."

David hugged her and said, "I do too. Let's get home and do this."

*

They were at the KOA in Lubbock again. The manager remembered them. They each got a one room cabin, no bathrooms or kitchen, but showers and laundry facilities were on site. They checked in for one night and gathered their laundry to get ready for the next day.

They walked the grounds, exercised the dogs and put the washed laundry back in their luggage. Bishoff and Debbie thought it was fun chasing balls and working off their energy. David had brought the plastic bags to clean up after them.

David brought Bishoff over for Kit to entertain while he went into town to buy them something to eat. He still had dry dog food, so that wasn't an issue. She took care of the feeding while he was gone.

They ate hamburgers and French fries. She felt better than she had in a long time. They had a plan. David couldn't wait for them to get home and start looking for land. She didn't know where to start after they purchased the land, but she had David looking out for their best interest. That felt right.

*

They got home at 6:30pm, two days after leaving Ruidoso. David followed her home and carried in her luggage as well as Debbie's toys and bed. He then made her go through every room before he left for his house.

For the next two days Kit got her house back in order, paid bills, went grocery shopping, and did the many other things that needed taking care of. The third day, David called and wanted to look at two properties.

When David rang the doorbell; she was wearing a sweater, sturdy boots, jeans, and was ready to go.

They drove to the two different locations that Jack Quinn, David's realtor, was showing them today. One property was located three miles out of town, but it was only 8 acres, too small for the buildings David wanted to build. The second parcel of land had too many older buildings they would have to tear down. They needed at least 30+ acres with a clean slate to start their projects.

Three days later David called Kit; Jack had a new client who wanted to sell a 60-acre hunting ranch for $450,000. It has two spring-fed creeks, two hunting cabins and an apartment attached to the barn.

"Jack has a closing this morning, so he asked if we could go and said he would call me later."

They drove 8 miles out of town to the Eaton Ranch. She had seen Drew Eaton in town. He had moved there from Montana three years ago. He seemed to be a loner and didn't seek out conversation.

They shook hands with Drew, making small talk about the colder weather coming. Drew led them to his Jeep Wrangler and said he would show them the lay of the land. He had cattle in different fenced pastures, and the deer were plentiful. Drew told them the spring water was clear and cold and had never gone dry. Drew left 30 acres unimproved for the hunters. To David this meant they had extra land to expand and build on later. They drove to the barn; it was about 5000 square feet. David loved the size; it had a tack room, hay storage, Drew's tractor and other supplies. David saw where he could use this existing building to start the kennels. It was useful and he liked what he saw. The hunting cabins were 650 square feet each and made with the same materials as the barn. He was thinking housing facilities for trainers.

Once they finished their tour, David asked, "Drew, we need to talk about this; we are very impressed. Can you give us a chance to make an offer before you start showing the property again?"

"I'll give you tonight and then I will have to go on. I've already purchased a place in the hill country and want to move as soon as I can."

Later, David and Kit were talking over each other in the car.

"I'm sorry." David explained, "I'm so pleased with that piece of property."

They couldn't wait to get to Kit's house and put the figures on paper.

*

"I know this is the place for us, what do you think?"

Kit could see the excitement on his face; it was contagious, "Yes, I can see the 60 acres is what we need."

David smiled, "Should we make an offer right now and start calling architects and contractors? I would like to make the full price offer of $450,000. The land alone will be worth that amount in a few years. Should I call Jack? What do you think?"

He was always thoughtful to include Kit in all parts of the 50/50 project. It wasn't just his adventure; it was hers, too.

"Call your realtor. How will we work the money from both of us? I will use the money Clare left me, if that's alright with you? That way I won't have to liquidate anything."

David smiled at her. "Look, I have the down payment, no problem, let's lock in the sale. Then we can go to an attorney, draw up a contract and go see a banker for our line of credit."

Drew accepted their full offer, and the loan process started. They would be closing in 45 days. The days were filled with getting assets available, signing papers, talking with builders, and finalizing the architect's blueprints of the new gymnasium and the renovation of the existing barn. Their line of credit from the bank allowed them to get the project completed.

Building the first set of kennels in the existing barn was first priority. David knew what he wanted and settled on a 5,000 square foot gymnasium, much like the one Drew constructed for the barn, with a red metal roof and light brick skirting with white metal siding. It would have a total of twenty dog cages, ten to a side. Half of each cage would be inside and the other half outside. He wanted chain-linked fencing outside the individual cages for the dog to take care of business. David wanted a door that could be shut at night, closing the dog off to the outside, so each night the dogs would be closed to the elements. The inside cage would have a dog bed and water.

There would be fenced-in areas for dog training and exercise outside around the dog kennel. The gym would be used for inside training and agility platforms. Later, they would build a small metal building for grooming where the public could bring their pets to be groomed, too.

David's self-esteem and self-respect went through the roof. He felt this goal they had set in motion could be accomplished in this next year.

They discussed the risk involved with taking on a project of this size. If a worst case scenario happened, David already had investors wanting to help them. As soon as the office was up and operating, they would start applying for grants available for shelter and rescue facilities. Within a week of closing, the project was on the move.

*

David and Kit were having a special dinner to celebrate and talk about what their positions would be in the organization and to finalize the name.

Kit told David she was preparing a dinner to celebrate. "So bring Bishoff and something to drink."

She was cooking chicken-fried steak, mashed potatoes with gravy, black-eyed peas, cornbread, sweet tea, and pecan pie for dessert. She was talking to Debbie as she put the chicken-fried steaks in the oven to stay warm.

"There's nothing better than a southern dinner with sweet tea for easing the hard decisions."

David and Bishoff showed up bearing gifts. Debbie and Bishoff each received a large bone; they would be entertained for the evening. When dinner was ready, they brought the meal to the table.

"It smells wonderful."

"Thanks, I hope it tastes as good as it smells."

They brought their glasses together and both said, "The In-Between Dog Academy."

They laughed; the name felt right.

David asked, "How will people find us online?"

Kit commented, "With the words dog and academy in the name, the correct server to throw us out to the net, and picking the right key words, it might work. Plus, we will be advertising in larger towns for skilled trainers to apply for the position here."

David smiled, "We can't go wrong trying to help people and dogs."

They didn't want the meal silent or awkward. David talked mostly to bring Kit up-to-date with the construction progress, telling her about the wooden molds that were made to pour the concrete slab for the gym.

Kit filled him in on picking the furnishings for the cabins and the apartment. "I'm pleased, the cabins and apartment furnishings needed to be updated, and, besides, they smelled like the hunters."

David smiled at Kit. She recognized "that look"; he knew something.

"I have been thinking of a plan for us. I'm going to move into one of the cabins. That way I will be there to answer questions and be available for the construction manager and service providers for different phases of the project. Kit, we could really make this an adventure. You wouldn't have to buy a cabin in the mountains. Look at this place of ours, waking up in the country every morning, seeing deer on the grounds, walking the dogs along the winding springs, literally working for ourselves to make this dream come true. We already have two cabins. I need you to take care of the phones being installed, interviewing and putting together the rest of our team, and the many other things that have to be done."

He stopped and leaned back in his chair and didn't say anything else. He could see the wheels turning in her head.

She took the moment to gather her thoughts. "I think that would be a great adventure with you as my partner. I know the dogs would love it, and we could really help each other reach our goals. Would we shut down our houses in town?"

David picked up steam now that he thought she might agree. "Yes, that's what I will do for the time being. There will come a time that we will come back to town; then the cabins would be available for trainees and trainers. Or, we could build other cabins and stay. The cabins are nice, cozy, and just enough space to really feel like home. At my house, I have so many rooms I never go in and sometimes just roam from room to room. We will still have the one-bedroom efficiency at the back of the barn. We could put bunk beds in the bedroom for the trainers."

Kit was beginning to feel the momentum and the strength she drew from David. She knew this was the time she had waited for all her life; once again, a leap-of-faith that she and David would be okay with this new life in front of them.

"Yes, I would like that. When can we start moving?"

He laughed, "Right after we have a piece of pie."

10

Kit woke to a new day, and she had something to do: pack. There was so much stuff to consider. She decided for the time being she wouldn't take any dishes; the cabin was furnished with everything. She spent all day sorting and packing the necessities, thinking "I want to take my own linens and bathroom items."

By three o'clock she had everything she needed and, if not, she could always come back to her house and pack more. It wasn't like living in Ruidoso two days away.

David was coming at three-thirty. She couldn't believe since last night their plans had gone to the next level. They were spending their first night on their land, in their very own cabins.

"Debbie, how exciting is this?"

Debbie was jumping around, also caught up in the excitement and packing frenzy. She barked once when Kit picked up her bed to put it in the trunk of the car.

The next day was Sunday, a good breathing point. Monday would be a working day, but for the next two days, she would take a break. She didn't have time to think if all this meant something personally with David.

She looked at Debbie and said, "If I don't dance with failure, how I will ever know joy? And that other saying, I have to know where I've been, to know where I'm going. Unknown authors."

Debbie thought it meant cookie time. For the time being, Kit would put one foot in front of the other.

David had traded his car in and bought a new super-cab pickup that morning. Bishoff was leaning out the passenger window, slobbering down the side. In the back David had four boxes, a suitcase, a small Bar-B-Que pit, and a cooler.

"I like your new pickup. I might do the same, trade in my car for a medium-sized truck."

He had room for all her stuff in back. He commented, as he hoisted the last box in the back, "I stopped and got two steaks, charcoal, and stuff for a salad, and I packed a couple of beers that had been left in my refrigerator. I think we're ready."

Kit walked up to David and in a flash she stood on her tip toes and kissed him on the cheek. "Thanks for making this dream come true."

David smiled, "You're welcome."

They followed each other out of town, smiling to themselves.

*

David had been busy since last night. He had called a cleaning agency to meet him at the cabins early this morning and clean the two cabins and apartment. He had taken care of everything to make their first night a comfortable, memorable experience for Kit.

It was seven o'clock; they had unpacked, and David put the steaks on the small charcoal grill he had set up downdraft between the cabins. Drew had built a picnic table with benches for his hunters to make camp. Kit brought a vinyl tablecloth from the Ruidoso trip she never used. The table was set and ready. They remade a small fire pit out of creek rocks gathered by the hunters during the last three years.

Kit had always enjoyed having an outside fire to stare into as she solved the world's problems. She also enjoyed listening to the locusts busting out to become something entirely different, and to the bull frog's lonely croak in hopes of a female returning his call. All together they had a natural, calming effect. She was glad she came.

Debbie and Bishoff thought gathering sticks for them to play with was a divine idea. Once the fire was started, the dogs moved off to the edge of darkness to chew on a couple of sticks.

David brought out the two beers from the cooler. "Might as well relax until the steaks are ready. So what do you think so far?" He casually tossed the question out to see what she would say.

"I love it. I can't believe we did all this since last night. Well, mostly you made everything happen."

"Don't kid yourself! I think it took you to plant this idea in my head. It just seemed right for us to move out here to make the best of this adventure. I'm glad we're here, Kit."

She felt warmed by the fire and liked the contentment they shared being together.

*

The first month was fast and furious. There were so many lists to concentrate on and complete. Kit traded her car for a medium-sized truck. Evansville Design and Decor Center contractors came to hang the new drapes, and she had the old mattresses replaced with new fresh ones. She felt better with the smelly, fireplace-smoked drapes and hunter mattresses gone. A fresh coat of white paint went a long way on updates for both cabins and apartment.

Each evening they still met at the picnic table to share their news of the day. The gym's concrete slab had been poured, cured, and was ready for the framing crew. The existing barn had the updated apartment on the south end; the kennel had twenty cages, ten to a side. On the north end was a small tack room with barrels of dog food, grooming tools, dog bowls and an enclosed dog shower. The first to try the shower were Debbie and Bishoff.

Kit's grandfather, Pa Pa Carson, had many idioms he used to tell her growing up. Some had stuck, like: "It doesn't cut the mustard, Kit." That meant she would have to do it over again and make it better. She looked up the phrase online a few years ago. It meant, genuine article or to reach or surpass. The definition explained that a long time ago mustard was fermented in barrels, and the top layer of the mustard had a hardened crust that had to be cut through. The blade had to be strong enough to cut through the hardened layer. She saw David and herself as "cutting the mustard."

Kit was waiting patiently for David this evening. She wanted to tell him about the three applications for trainers that she had received from their Dallas-based Public Relations Company: Weir, Donnelly and Wakefil. Kit had researched several advertising firms, and she liked what she read and their reviews.

She and David couldn't accomplish everything they wanted to with just the two of them. They wanted to delegate parts of the responsibilities to others who would help take them to the next level.

David was walking down the dirt road to the cabins. The sun was going down behind him and she swore he looked like Clint Eastwood after a hard day of saving the West.

"Whoa, Kit, get a grip," she thought.

He looked up and saw her at the picnic table; the soft, glowing light before twilight was on her face and hair. She had a confident look about her tonight.

He smiled to himself, thinking, "This is the way to spend my retirement, doing something I love and with someone I think I have fallen in love with over this last year. We took an idea from nothing to helping dogs get to where they are supposed to be with humans."

He walked to her and said, "Hi, country girl."

"Hey, yourself. This has been an amazing week for me, how about yourself?"

"Would it be okay if I change clothes and get us a couple beers out of the refrigerator? It's pot luck as far as the beer goes. I know Big John said he put a few in for us."

"By all means, Mr. Eastwood, I will start the fire in the pit."

He slightly turned his head towards her, looking at her sideways as he walked towards his cabin. The element of surprise, that's one of the things he had always liked about Kit, always keeping him guessing. And where did she get all the off-beat humor? Comparing him to Clint Eastwood was okay with him.

"What a difference your handy work can make in a short time, Kit. I like my cabin and it smells clean." He smiled, handing her a beer when he returned.

"I'm glad you like it. Freshness never hurt anything. We have to be careful for a couple of weeks until the cabinet paint has dried, or 'cured' as my grandmother called it."

Sitting down, he commented, "The swimming pool is ready for a dip. I want to check the filter system to make sure the dog hair isn't going to clog the works. There will be a lot of dogs swimming later. I will stick to gym shorts and a t-shirt."

She smiled, "Sounds like a man with a plan."

They talked about the updates and what their goals were for the next week. Kit told him about the two applicants.

David said, "Once we have hired two trainers, we will be ready to start receiving the first dogs when they become available from the Academy. We need to hire staff employees to take care of the feeding, watering, etc."

Kit remarked, "I would like to hire local help for the staff, if that's alright with you? Support our town when we can."

She continued with her update, "I have a landscaping team coming Monday to cut the grass and clear the property around the house, and Evansville Pest control is coming that afternoon to spray the property inside and out, with animal-friendly products." She wanted to make sure there were no snakes or varmints near their property. "The office and reception area will be ready next week."

He asked, "Would it be alright next Sunday afternoon if we gave a Bar-B-Que for the workers and their families? They can go swimming, eat and play. I will tell them they can bring their dogs if they play nice. Their kids could run around. They're good workers, and they understand the significance of this special place, our In-Between Dog Academy. I let them put their names in the poured concrete around the grounds. Sounds silly, but it meant something to them. Some signed their own name, but most put their family name: Rubin signed, Rubin Reyes Family, then there was the Waller Bunch and, of course, Big John."

They laughed; Big John had been with them since the beginning of construction.

"Yes, I like that idea. It would be fun to try everything out. Are we catering or cooking?"

"I would like to get the meat catered from town. I'm making Velveeta cheese dip with Rotel, straight from the microwave. I can also make a mean potato salad."

She laughed, "Okay, I'm calling Dorothy at the Heavenly Bakery for dessert, and I can bring my big pots from town to cook the beans and a couple of slow cookers to keep the dip warm."

They discussed the need to buy a van for transporting the dogs and a gazillion other things. They had picked a dog food company that would deliver. Dog food was important to them, some of the dog food would be no grain for dogs with allergies and another was high protein for the younger dogs.

They turned in early that night; both were worn out from the week. Kit was propped up on a bunch of new pillows, writing a list of groceries. She stopped, thinking, "David and I have grown close this year working together."

They had let each other accomplish goals in their own right. "He lets me do my thing. The wheels of success are rolling along, 'r-o-l-l-l-i-n-g-on-the-r-i-v-e-r,'" she sang to Debbie on her bed. "If I were to think about it; I might have fallen in love with David from the moment he walked in the door of the condo in Ruidoso." Now that was a thought: she had never been in love and here she was in her sixties. She wondered how he felt.

Meanwhile, David was sitting at the table staring at nothing. "Why didn't I say something to her tonight? I feel this is right between us. She's smart, witty, and rises to this adventure with me."

He went to bed thinking he would say something to her after the picnic.

11

"Yes, I'm sure, Dorothy. I want one hundred cupcakes. Half of the cupcakes should have cream icing and the others chocolate. Do you bake dog cookies?"

"No, but I'll bet I can find a recipe. How many will you need?"

"Let's say a total of fifty in small, medium, and large. If this goes over well, I will want to order more for the store we will be opening."

"Thank you, Kit. That would help me a lot."

She was in town buying the bulk of the groceries they would need for next Sunday. She had a long list to buy. She marked through each item as she went down the aisles. She marked off pinto beans, chips, mustard, ketchup, and the stuff for the potato salad. Onstadt Catering would provide the paper plates, pickles, onions, and bar-b-que sauce. She had gone by the bakery and paid for the order, and she stopped by her house to get pots for the beans and her two crock pots. She and David would grill hamburgers tonight.

She did most of the cooking, and David did the grilling. He was in town making plans with the Bar-B-Que Master, Carl Onstadt, owner of Onstadt Catering.

*

She had been gone for five hours

"Should I be worried and call her or just sit tight?" He thought he would just touch base with her. "Kit, are you okay? You've been gone a long time."

"Hey, thanks for calling. I'm almost done, but you are going to have to help me unload. I should be there in thirty minutes. Start a fire please, because we are having hamburgers."

They hung up. David knew he had done the right thing by calling, and Kit felt a new pleasant feeling about David, knowing he cared.

They were hanging around the fire after eating and talking about the Van they needed. "Yes, let me take care of the Van. I need you to hire a receptionist ASAP."

Kit smiled, "We can mark that one off our list. Do you know Cathy Weathersby in town?" He shook his head no. "She is our new receptionist starting Monday; she can help keep us organized. I saw her as I was loading the truck at the supermarket. She walked over to say hello and laughed when she saw all the groceries. She asked why I was buying out the store. I told her what was going on, and she said if we needed any help she was looking. Cathy had been a bank teller and lost her job because of cutbacks a couple months ago. I told her I didn't need to call, come in Monday at 10 o'clock. She was ecstatic. One more thing accomplished."

The week was full of long days trying to get everything done for the party Sunday.

David told her Thursday night, "I honestly think we are going to pull this off."

Kit said, "Tomorrow I'm putting the beans in the refrigerator to soak overnight. I will start cooking them Saturday. I brought my large pots and two crock pots from home to keep your dip warm."

David said he was going to cook the potato salad Saturday also. "Potato salad always tastes better after being in the refrigerator overnight; that way I can tweak it Sunday morning."

Both were happy to show the workers what they had helped to build. Most importantly, they wanted to show them what people can accomplish if they are kind and work together for a mutual goal.

*

It was Sunday and celebration time. People would be arriving for the party. David and Kit had early morning coffee on her porch before the festivities began.

"We have accomplished all of this within a short period of time. I still can't believe we put this together from your dream. I guess it's time; are you ready?"

She laughed, "Let the party begin."

They didn't get to talk again. The swimming pool was a big splash for the kids and their pets. David and Big John had set up a volley ball net on the grounds. Onstadt Catering had set up the tables and chairs this morning when they delivered the Bar-B-Que. Kit was overseeing the tables of food with Cathy. She had been with them a week and loved her job. Kit was pleased with the outcome, and the dog cookies and cupcakes were going to be a big hit. David was keeping track of the kids in the pool and Big John was trying to keep up with the kids and pets on the grounds.

At twelve o'clock, Kit whistled, "Alright, everyone out and dry off, the food's ready!"

The kids were the first to swamp the tables. Kids were always hungry. She and Cathy put the dog treats at the end of each table.

Kit tapped a metal spoon against a metal container of tea and said loudly, "Don't forget to give your pets a treat before you eat; it gives them something to eat while we eat."

Everyone laughed.

David stood up and began, "Thank you for coming. Kit had a dream one night about starting an in-between shelter for dogs that have been trained at the Dog Academy here and at other Texas dog academies. Once the trainer graduates, the animal will come here. We want to make this a win-win situation. We are here to help on many different levels. We are going to help people and well-trained dogs come together. We are hiring skilled trainers and personnel to get us to that level. Everyone here helped and we are appreciative. Thanks again. Let's eat!"

Everyone started leaving around 4 o'clock, saying their goodbyes and wishing them luck. Kit was passing out more dog treats to take home. The men helped David take down the tables and stack the chairs for Onstadt Catering to pick up the next day.

David told her he was going to feed Debbie and Bishoff and would meet her at the picnic table in thirty minutes. Kit wanted to refresh and change her clothes.

"What a wonderful day." Kit couldn't be happier.

"We deserve this," he said. David smiled, and she could tell he had something on his mind. "I have wanted to talk to you about us."

She waited. "We have talked about knowing each other most of our lives. So you know I'm not a bad person. I would like to think we are more than just friends by now."

Now it was his turn to wait. "I have been thinking about the same thing. I would like to know where this leads us."

"Alright," he said, "we need to take some time for us. How about next Sunday we go into town and call it a date."

She smiled, "Sounds like a man with a plan, and, yes, that would be wonderful."

12

David and Kit worked hard over the next year. They hired trainers to start a training facility for dog trainees, and their growing office and behind-the-scenes staff had been hired locally as they promised. Cathy, the office manager, made sure pictures of dogs in training were posted on their website and social media for adoption. The Pro Dog Shop and dog grooming facilities were a hit with the locals, and they had leased modular homes to house new trainers and trainees. The In-Between Dog Academy had been awarded grants for their continued efforts of training and rescuing animals. Kit and David were pleased the local senior citizens saw their vision and were coming daily to pick a trained pet companion.

They had a plan to get into the service-dog aspect of the business, but that would take time. The average training period for a service dog is two years. Their trainers had told Kit and David that only one in hundred dogs were special enough to train to become a service dog. They had also learned that for a Veteran to adopt a service dog it would cost the Veteran $40,000. They wanted to help with that situation. Their personal constitution was still based on trained dogs being matched with humans in a forever home.

One Sunday night, after yet another successful week at the Academy, they decided to go out to a nice dinner at Majestic Meals on the Plaza. Chef Pierre had transformed this small German-style 1880's retail building into a quaint restaurant and bar. Customers were delighted to be led to the back patio, where they heard soft classical music and dined among small, white twinkling lights with white linen table cloths and candles.

David had been hoping Kit would approve of the restaurant.

She said, "I love this restaurant. The Chef is known for his surprises: order a hamburger, and it might come with deliciously grilled vegetables and the meat arrives flaming to be gently placed on toasted buns."

He laughed, and she went on, "Chef Pierre is adorable and he is the reason this restaurant is so popular."

They both ordered the fresh grilled tuna. This dinner was special. They took their time eating, laughing and smiling across the table at one another. Chef Pierre came to wish them happiness on their business and told them the Champagne was on him.

After dinner, they held hands walking to their car.

David was looking at Kit, "Here, let's sit on this bench for a minute. This has been a happy occasion to celebrate. Are you happy, Kit?"

She squeezed his hand, "Yes, I think we mesh together well. We both have the same goals and they are worthwhile, but more than that, I love you, David."

David removed a small box from his pocket. "This was my mother's engagement ring from my dad. I would like you to wear it."

Kit didn't expect this, "I would be honored to wear your mother's engagement ring."

David kept going, "This is a promise to you; I will always be emotionally available for you and be there during your darkest hours. I've got your back. That's all I can ask in return."

Kit smiled and said, "And don't forget; I accept your craziness, if you accept my craziness."

They laughed.

He put the ring on her left ring finger. She looked at him, "I think Clare would approve. Did you know she asked me to look after you?"

"She asked me the same thing, to look after you." He took both of her hands and brought her to stand in front of him. "I'm in love with you, Kit."

She came right back, "I love you."
He kissed her and she kissed him back.
On the way home that night, even if they were in their sixties, he pulled in a rest stop, stopped the car and pulled her to him, saying, "I love you. We are going to have a wonderful life together."

Dear Readers

I was finishing *Dear Old Dogs* when Hurricane Harvey struck Houston, Texas on August 12th, 2017. I couldn't stop watching TV and the heroic happenings between humans and animals. It gave me hope about our world saving each other and all the animals that help us get through the worst of times. Every human being deserves another chance at life and every pet deserves a forever home.

I wrote this novel because Kit Carson and David Bishop had a tragedy happen in their lives and wanted to help people and animals connect. They thought the "In-Between Dog Academy" they built was an effective way for both humans and animals to find each other and comfort one another.

I would love to hear from you. Visit my website, gwenhead.com, and leave me a message.

About Atmosphere Press

Atmosphere Press is an independent full-service publisher for books in genres ranging from non-fiction to fiction to poetry, with a special emphasis on being an author-friendly approach to the often-brutal challenges of getting a book into the world. Learn more about what we do at Atmosphere's website, atmospherepress.com.

And of course, we encourage you to check out some of Atmosphere's latest releases, which are available at Amazon.com, BarnesandNoble.com, and via order from your local bookstore:

Ghost Sentence, poems by Mary Flanagan
What Outlives Us, poems by Larry Levy
Bello the Cello, a children's book by Dennis Mathew
That Beautiful Season, a novel by Sandra Fox Murphy

What I Cannot Abandon, poems by William
    Guest
Such a Nice Girl, a novel by Carol St. John
All the Dead Are Holy, poems by Larry Levy
How Not to Sell, nonfiction by Rashad Daoudi
Surviving Mother, a novella by Gwen Head
Rescripting the Workplace, nonfiction by Pam
    Boyd
Winter Park, a novel by Graham Guest

About Gwen Head

Gwen Head is a native Texan born in 1947. She decided on her sixtieth birthday she would complete the novel she had started writing for caregivers while her mother was living with her battling Alzheimer's Disease. This book was called *Surviving Mother*.

Her second novel, *Lone Wolf: Tales of an Independent Biker* is a collection of true stories about her husband's life in Austin running a security company for the world-famous Armadillo World Headquarters and Willie Nelson Picnics.

This is Gwen's third novel. This novel reflects the lifetime relationships we have with our friends and pet companions. She adopted the real Debbie from a dog academy in the Austin area. This is a work of fiction, but it could happen. It all starts with an idea.

Gwen lives thirty miles from Austin, Texas with her Bernese Mountain dog, Buddy. Her beloved pet companion Debbie passed away in 2017. Gwen will continue storytelling about life and the curves it throws us. Enjoy.

www.ingramcontent.com/pod-product-compliance
Lightning Source LLC
Chambersburg PA
CBHW032253070726
47590CB00016B/2637